THE STABLE CAT'S Christmas

For Mom and Dad, who
believed it could happen.
　　　　　　　—C.S.V.

To my wonderful family, for being
such a fantastic support and just
for being there—love you all.
　　　　　　　—G.Y.

ISBN-13: 978-0-8249-5683-7

Published by WorthyKids/Ideals
An imprint of Worthy Publishing Group
A division of Worthy Media, Inc.
Nashville, Tennessee

Text copyright © 2017 by Christina S. Vrba
Art copyright © 2017 by Worthy Media, Inc.

Library of Congress CIP data on file

Designed by Georgina Chidlow-Irvin

Printed and bound in China
RRD-SZ_Jul17_1

THE STABLE CAT'S
Christmas

WRITTEN BY
Christina S. Vrba

ILLUSTRATED BY
Gail Yerrill

WorthyKids
ideals®

Nashville, Tennessee

here once was a dusty, hay-smelling stable behind an old inn in the town of Bethlehem. When travelers came to the inn, their horses and donkeys went into the stable.

But none of the animals stayed for long
in the stable except the innkeeper's cow, a few
doves, and one small, plain, sand-colored cat
who kept the mice and rats away.

One night, as the little cat returned
from a prowl, she heard voices in the stable.
There in the shadows, she saw a tired woman
and a kind-eyed man. They smiled down at
something small nestled in the woman's arms.

The cat also saw the shepherds from the fields kneeling close by and, lying just outside the door, the shepherds' dog.

"Hello, Dog," said the cat, greeting him warmly. "Who is this in our stable? Why are your shepherds here?"

"Haven't you heard?" asked the dog. "A child, a great king, has been born—right here in this stable!"

"A king!" marveled the cat. "But I thought kings lived in palaces, not stables! I would like to see him. Dog, where is he?"

"He is just inside," said the dog. "He is very
small—but oh, Cat, he looked at me and smiled!
Angels told my masters that he will bring peace to
all the world. We came to see him and offer him gifts."

The little cat felt a bit sad, for she wanted to see this king. But she needed a gift. She padded into the stable. There she found the friendly cow.

"He is just inside," said the dog. "He is very small—but oh, Cat, he looked at me and smiled! Angels told my masters that he will bring peace to all the world. We came to see him and offer him gifts."

"But I have no gift to give," said the cat. "I am only a cat. And you are only a dog—what gift can a dog give to a king?"

"I will guard the child and his mother as they sleep," said the shepherds' dog. "It is a good gift for a dog to give."

It is a good gift, thought the cat.

But I cannot guard the child. I am only a cat.

The little cat felt a bit sad, for she wanted to see this king. But she needed a gift. She padded into the stable. There she found the friendly cow.

"Cow," asked the cat, "is what the dog says true? Is this child in our stable a king? Have you brought a gift as well?"

"Yes, the dog speaks the truth," said the cow. "The child sleeps in my manger, and when morning comes, I will be waiting with warm milk."

"I have no manger and no milk," said
the cat. "What gift can I possibly give?"

The little cat felt even sadder than before and crept deep into the stable. She tucked her tail around her and stared glumly at her paws.

"Here, now," said a voice. "What's wrong?"

The little cat looked up and saw an old donkey watching her.

"Oh, Donkey, I have heard of the newborn child, the great king. The dog protects him. The cow gives her manger and her milk. I want to see him, but I have no gift."

"Nonsense," said the donkey. "We all have gifts. I have a strong back and careful feet. I carried the child's mother all the long way here. That is my gift.

"Look inside your heart, Cat. You have a gift—you need only to find it."

The little cat thought and thought. *Could the donkey's words be true?*

All grew quiet and still in the stable. The cat looked around.

I may not have a gift, she thought, *but I can wish the child well.*

She made her way on silent paws to where the child slept.

How small he is! thought the cat. *How little, and how new! I do wish I had a gift for him.*

At that moment, the little cat noticed something: the baby was shivering!

And without thinking, she slipped into the manger beside the child. She pressed her warm fur against him. The shivering stopped.

The cat closed her eyes and lay her head on her paws. She felt a gentle stirring. She looked up—and the child looked back at her, smiling!

He reached out to stroke her, his tiny, gentle fingers making tracks through her thick fur.

The cat leaned into the child's touch.
But when she glanced over her shoulder,
she blinked in surprise!

Everywhere the child had touched, and
all over her coat, were lovely golden-orange
stripes! The little cat purred with joy and pride.

And so, from that first Christmas Day to this, all tabby cats wear those same stripes on their own coats.

And they remember a small, nameless, sand-colored cat who shared a gift from the heart, for a very special little king named *Jesus.*